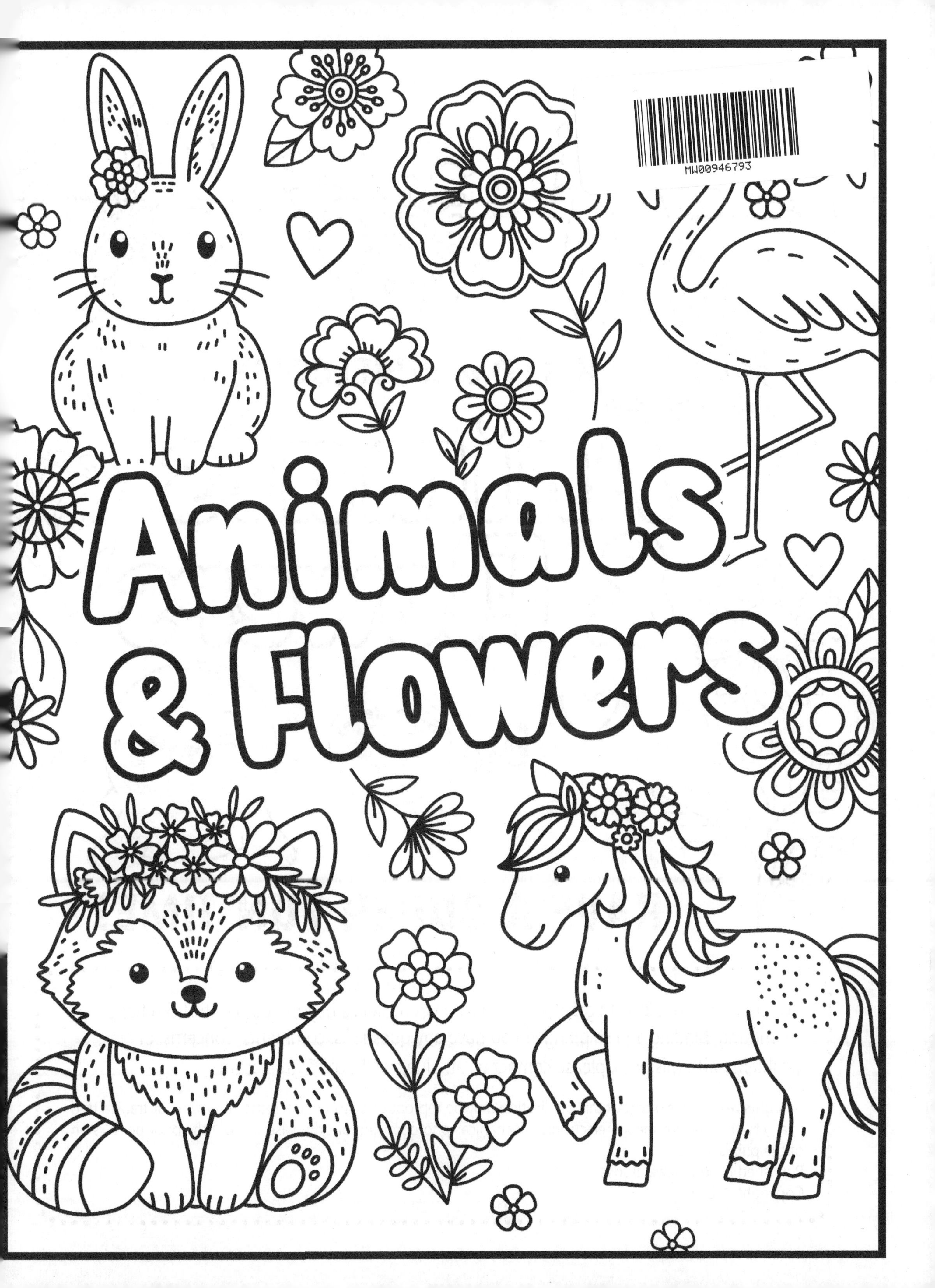
Animals
& Flowers
MW00946793

HAVE A SUPER FUN TIME!

We create our books with great love and care yet mistakes beyond our control can happen in printing, binding and shipping. If you have any questions, comments, concerns, or problems with this book please contact us at: bluejewelbooks@gmail.com.

Published by Blue Jewel Books

Bonus: Learn to Draw Cute Flower Doodles

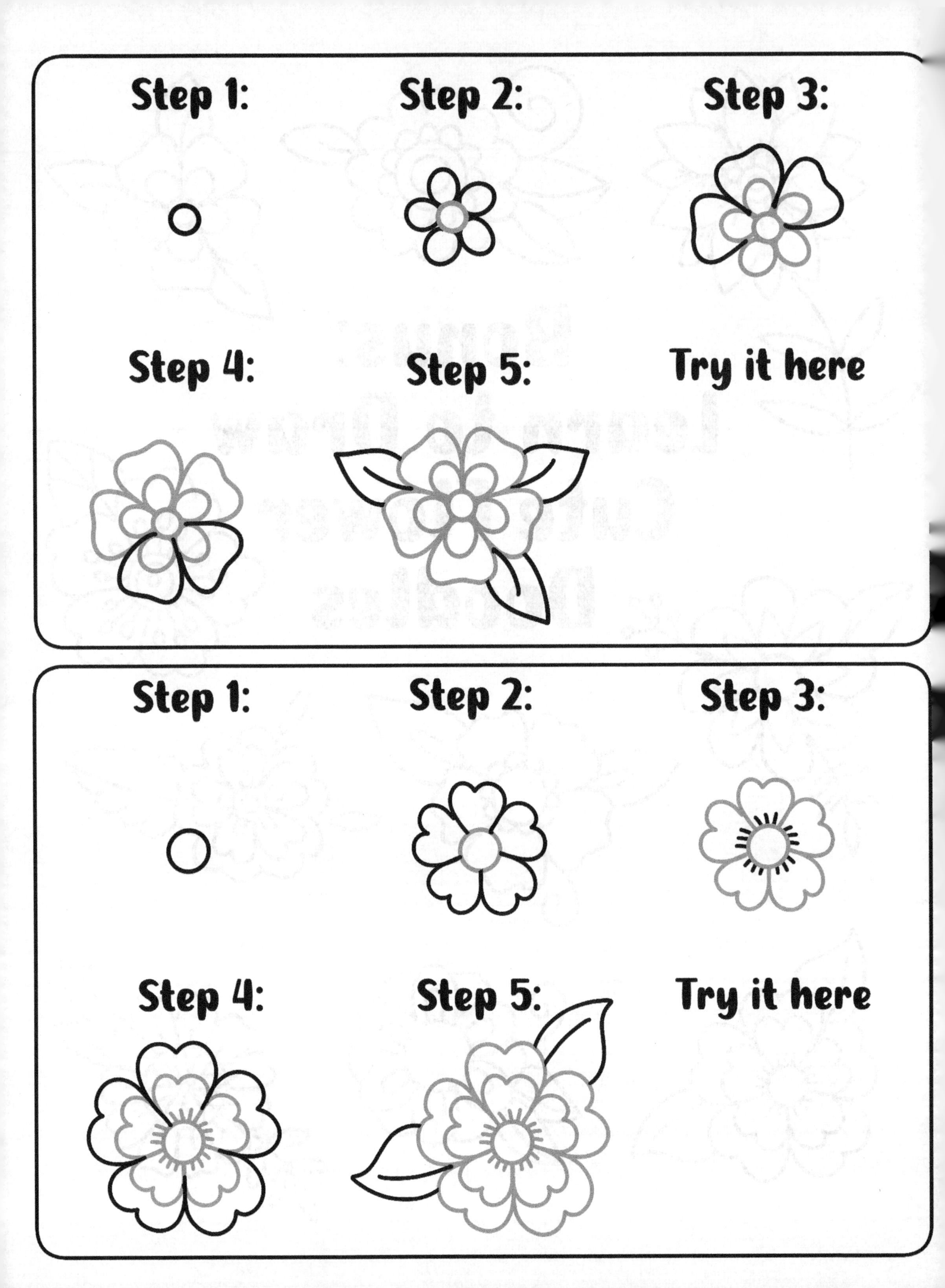
Step 1:
Step 2:
Step 3:
Step 4:
Step 5:
Try it here
Step 1:
Step 2:
Step 3:
Step 4:
Step 5:
Try it here

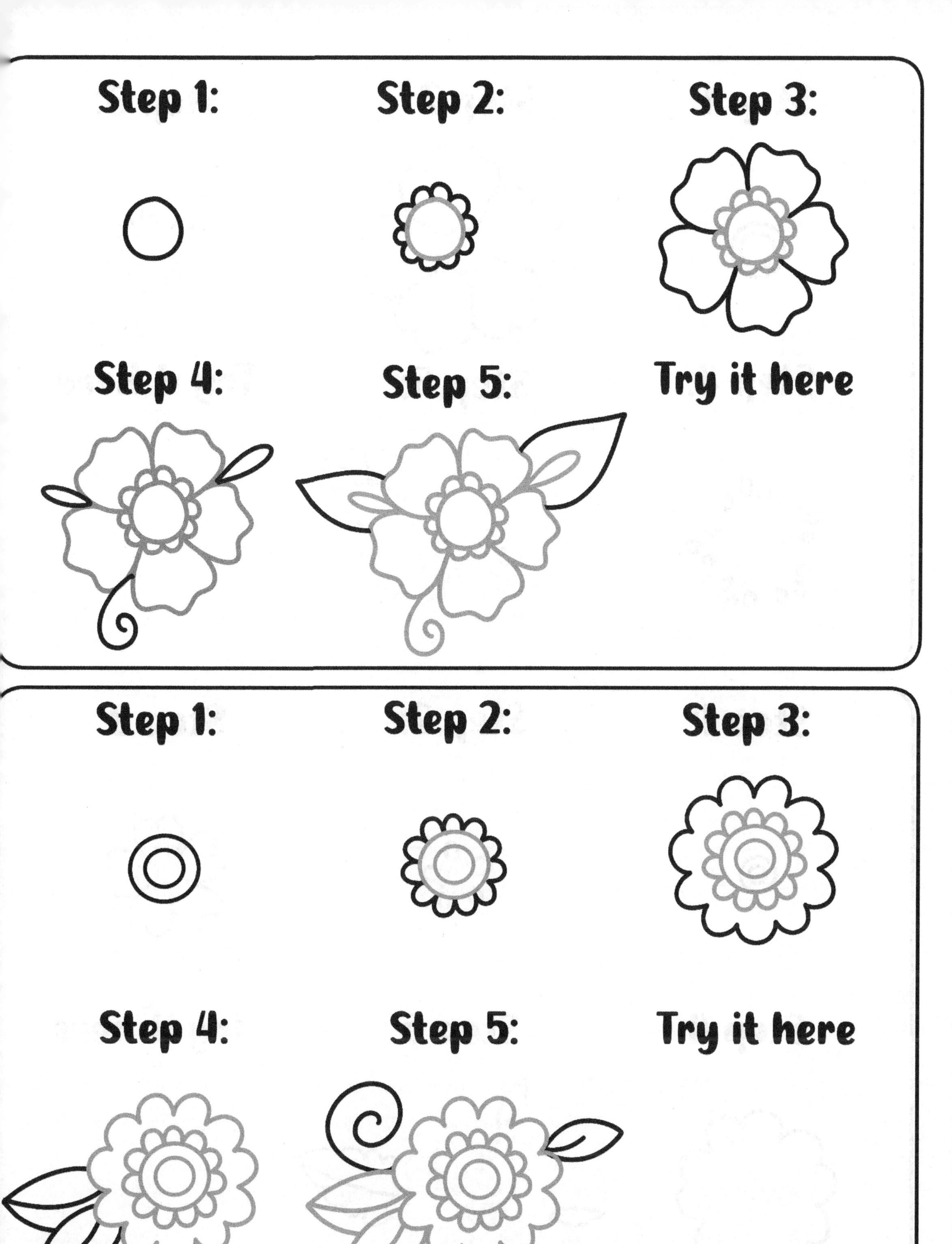
Step 1:
Step 2:
Step 3:
Step 4:
Step 5:
Try it here
Step 1:
Step 2:
Step 3:
Step 4:
Step 5:
Try it here

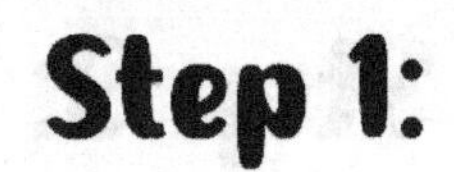

Step 1:

Step 2:

Step 3:

Step 4:

Step 5:

Try it here

Step 1:

Step 2:

Step 3:

Step 4:

Step 5:

Try it here

Step 1:

Step 2:

Step 3:

Step 4:

Step 5:

Try it here

Step 1:

Step 2:

Step 3:

Step 4:

Step 5:

Try it here

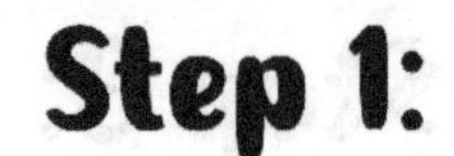

Step 2:

Step 3:

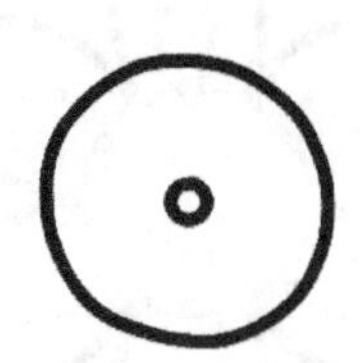

Step 4:

Step 5:

Try it here

Step 1:

Step 2:

Step 3:

Step 4:

Step 5:

Try it here

Made in the USA
Las Vegas, NV
12 December 2024